RECRUIT'S PADDED FIRST TIME

Steamy ABDL MM Story

Jerry Hastings

ISBN: 9798802115862
Imprint: Independently published

1st edition

Cover design by: Jerry Hastings

CONTENTS

CHAPTER 1

"You are a lost cause," said Sgt. Andrew Frost, stepping toward me and putting himself right behind me. He placed his right hand over mine, lifting my arm so that the rifle was better positioned against my shoulder. I could feel his body coming closer to mine, making me feel tingles all over. He was slightly older than me, tanned, muscular, and imposing.

It would be a lie to say that I could do anything to stop what was going on.

And what was going on wasn't sufficient, I could tell when he pressed his groin against me, rubbing his cock and balls on me. I had no idea if he was doing those things on purpose, but it was getting incredibly hard to focus on anything else that wasn't satisfying my sexual fantasies.

Sgt. Andrew Frost was also a little taller than me, which only helped with making me feel more submissive than I already was. When I signed up for the Army, I didn't think I was going to find myself under the command of such a hot and demanding man. He had no idea that I was gay and if it were up to me, he would continue being oblivious to it.

His hand was slightly callous, moving over mine and cupping it. I could feel his finger pressing against mine and guiding it to where the trigger was. He lowered his head, moving it so that it was right by the side of my head. He was breathing slowly and I could feel his hot breath against my face, which was only making things worse.

It was a good thing that the uniform the Army gave me was baggy enough to hide the raging boner in my pants. Otherwise, it wouldn't be just Sgt. Andrew Frost that would be noticing that and making fun of me. If anything, the whole motherfucking Army of the United States would be bullying me, and that wasn't something I wanted to be thinking about right now.

And one of the reasons behind that was the fact that in my spare time, when nobody was looking, I enjoyed roleplaying as a little. It was something innocent and quite naïve, but still something that could put my life at risk. Most of all, I didn't want to do anything that could endanger the stream of income that came from the Army.

"You are supposed to press the trigger like this," he said, his voice slightly lower than normal and with a hint of sensuality in it. I had no idea what was going on in his mind, but it just couldn't be what I was hoping it was, right?

"I'm trying, sergeant, but it's so difficult, especially when so many people are always looking at me and judging me," I said, realizing that I sounded more awkward than normal.

"That's why I'm here. I'm here to guide you, to do everything for you that you need," he murmured against my ear, making me feel another round of tingles all over my body.

My cock was just so hard right now it was poking against my pants, tenting it up slightly. One quick glance from one of my buddies in the Army and they would figure out what was going on.

"And lift the rifle slightly like this," he said again and this time I could feel his chest pressing against my back, making me feel warmer than I was. It was hot outside and yet I still knew that what I was feeling had little to do with that.

I just had no experience and I was always awkward around other men that I found out. And Sargent Andrew, now that he was over 30 years of age, was definitely hitting all the spots in me that made me feel like this.

But the glint of a ring on his finger showed me that he was married. I had no idea why I was even feeling that we had any chance of working, of becoming a couple, but it was obvious that

that was what my mind was hoping for. I was already thinking that, when I was in my bunk and it was dark, I would probably jerk off and come in my trousers, all the while my roommates had no idea about what was going on.

I was beginning to think that at least one of them was gay like me, but I never asked him anything about it and I wasn't going to, probably.

Regardless, it wasn't like those things mattered right now. What mattered was that this hunky beefcake had his body around me, making me feel so small, his skin against mine, and he was crossing every boundary possible.

Even the other officials in the Army were probably looking at us and wondering what was happening.

And yet, they weren't doing anything about it, probably because they were afraid of what Sgt. Andrew could do. The level of influence that he had in this local battalion was probably greater than anything they had combined.

"Thank you, Sgt Frost. You are helping me so much."

"And yet, I feel like it's not sufficient."

"What do you mean?" I asked, turning my eyes so that I could see him in the corner of my vision, feeling his beard now grazing my right cheek, which was yet one more thing I thought wasn't going to happen.

It was one thing keeping his body pressed up against me and another grazing his head against me, and it was so close that I could even smell the breath coming out of his mouth.

"How about coming to my room tonight so that I can give you some extra tips?"

I felt shivers running down my spine, and yet I knew that it was a decision that I alone should make. After all, he wasn't forcing me into doing anything, just that he was, as always, being extremely influential.

He placed his other hand against my left hand, making me move my arms slightly upward. The rifle was now comfortably pressed against my shoulder and I felt a lot more confident in my aiming ability this time. I supposed that that was the advantage of having Sgt. Andrew putting so much effort into making sure that I was learning.

"A little bit more to the side," he said and I turned the rifle in the direction that he wanted, soon finding out that the target was in the crosshairs and I could hit it without a problem.

Seconds later, I pressed the trigger and the rifle shot the bullet and pierced the plaque made of wood, and I finally felt Sgt. Andrew stepping away from me, which made me feel a little more comfortable and also slightly sad.

I turned around so that I was looking at him and I realized that he wasn't smiling in satisfaction like I thought he was going to be now that he knew that I was getting better at shooting. I was still a far cry from actually being deployed and shooting real, living targets, but that wasn't something that bothered me right now.

Nothing was bothering me right now, to be more precise. The only thing that was in the vicinity of my mind was his invitation to go to his office – or to be more accurate, his room – in the encampment. I had no idea what awaited me there, but I was excited. I couldn't wait to find out what he had in store for me.

It wasn't that I was thinking we were going to do anything prohibited together, but the possibility was still in the air and I couldn't stop thinking about it. And one more thing that just refused to go away from my mind right now was how I couldn't stop checking him out, every part of him being something that was part of my dreams - or was going to be, especially on the nights that were going to come.

I cleared my throat, realizing that the seconds were passing and Sgt. Andrew wasn't saying anything. He was just checking me out – or more like he was staring at me as if he could read what I was thinking.

But then, a moment later, he patted me on the shoulder and turned around after saying, "I'll be waiting for you in my room. I hope to see you there and that you don't disappoint me."

I saluted him, feeling my armpits wetter than they normally were. Actually, scratch that. It wasn't even the tip of the iceberg of everything that was happening to my body right now. I was so sweaty, so smelly, so sticky I thought that I could never go back to being my normal self.

Well, there was no point in delaying what needed to be done.

I tipped up my chin, went out of the training area, and then to the barracks. I guess that now I needed to continue my training and survive through it until it was dark.

CHAPTER 2

I could almost hear his voice speaking my name. Devin. He would say it over and over, calling out to me, even while it was still dark and everybody that was in the room could hear me.

I could hear the chirp of the crickets outside the room, some of the recruits snoring. My hand went under my trousers and I grabbed my cock, hoping that nobody was going to hear what I was going to do. Sgt. Andrew told me that I was supposed to go there in about 20 minutes and those were some of the most excruciating minutes of my life.

I started to stroke my dick slowly, picking up the pace just as slowly. I was in the first bunk bed and the guy that was sleeping on the bed above me couldn't hear me. At least, that's what I was telling myself as I continued to jerk off. It was a little risky, but certainly worth it.

If there was something that I hated now that I was in the Army, it was the fact that I couldn't play with my diapers and pretend that I was a little.

It was for that reason that I couldn't wait until this period of my life was over and I could go back to being my old self. I checked out the sides of what was around me, noticing that all the recruits were sleeping heavily. So much so that I could still hear them snoring, and it didn't look like that was going to change anytime soon.

In the meantime, I was imagining Sgt. Andrew popping into the room, catching me red-handed. He would deliver a harsh punishment for the infraction that I was committing and that wouldn't be even the tip of the iceberg. He would spank me, ground me, and I would be able to do nothing against that.

Then, when I was crying, he would hold me in his arms and comfort me without showing me much mercy. Was that too much to ask? I didn't know, but the thought was swirling in my mind and I couldn't brush it off.

My hand was now moving so fast it was a blur and it was a little irritating that I couldn't put my cock out of my pants. I wanted to do that, but I didn't want to risk one of the recruits opening their eyes and noticing that something was going on. If they as much as caught a whiff of what was happening, I would be screwed. So much so that I would have to leave the Army, which was something that, now that I was thinking about it, probably wasn't so bad.

It took no more than a minute until I was coming all over me, the smell of my come impregnating the air around me. It was only going to last a while, so I didn't worry about it. I just made sure that I grabbed my socks and cleaned myself up with them. Socks always smelled foul, so I didn't think that anybody in the sleeping quarters was going to notice that anything was amiss.

I checked my watch one more time on my wrist before sliding off the bed and then putting on an appropriate set of vestments so that I could walk around in this place without anyone suspecting that I was doing something wrong. We were allowed to go out of the sleeping quarters without drawing suspicion, so I should be okay. And yet, my heart was pounding in my chest, even though it was mostly because I had no idea what Sgt. Andrew was going to do with me when I was in his room.

I crossed several hallways before stopping in front of the door to his room, lifting my hand at the same moment when his voice boomed from the other side of it, "You can come in. The door is already unlocked."

I tried the doorknob and I wasn't surprised when it opened. I mean, I didn't think that he was going to lie, and especially not about something like that. After I opened the door, I found out that he was seated behind his desk, scribbling something on a piece of paper.

I stepped into the room and didn't know what to say, just keeping my hands clasped in front of me as if I was afraid they were going to do something without my permission and ruin the well-behaved guy façade that I was making use of right now.

Time passed and nothing happened, making me wonder what the hell was even going on in Sgt. Andrew's head. After a minute or so, he put away the piece of paper where he was scribbling something and then stepped toward me. It was at that moment, just like so many others before it, that I noticed he was taller than me.

He was with his hands clasped behind his back as he said, "You must be wondering right now why I asked you to come here."

I didn't know what to say, merely nodding and clearing my throat. He was just so hot, especially thanks to his piercing-blue eyes. It was like he could look straight into my soul thanks to those irises and pupils, I thought, feeling even more uncomfortable than normal.

"Well, you don't have to wonder any longer," he said, moving his hands up and then starting to undo the buttons of his shirt. He was still with his uniform on, and I had no idea why he was beginning to expose his chest to me.

"It's getting a little hot here, isn't it?" He asked, winking slowly.

After he lowered his hands after undoing the first buttons of his shirt at the top, he stepped toward me until he was no more than a couple of feet from bumping against me. I almost wondered if he was going to do that or if he was going to hug me, but then he didn't do anything. He was just there, checking me out, and making me feel as comfortable as I was turned on.

"Do you allow me to do this?" He asked, lifting his hand and putting it close to my shoulder, and this time I was surprised that he was asking for permission. All the other times when he touched me, he did so without doing anything resembling that. And it wasn't just my dick that was hard right now, but also my asshole that kept on clenching, almost as if it was protecting itself against something that might breach it. I had no idea if that was the case, but Sgt. Andrew was still making me feel so awkward.

And that, in turn, was hitting all the right spots in me.

I nodded and he placed his hand on my shoulder, asking, "And do you let me do this as well?"

He was suggesting that he wanted to move his hand around my body and, seeing what was happening, realizing that this was a dream happening right before my eyes, I had no choice but to nod again. That earned me a smile from him and he lowered his hands slightly further down, until they weren't on my arm anymore, but on my waist.

Just like all the other times, I had no idea what his intention was.

I thought that Sgt. Andrew was going to move his hand to the left and find my junk, perhaps even cup it too, but it appeared that he had other intentions in his mind, for he moved his hand away.

I lifted my eyebrows as I asked, without using words, what he was doing.

"You disappoint me."

"Why?" I croaked.

"You jerked off without my permission."

I gritted my teeth. The last thing I thought he was going to bring up was that. "I'm sorry. I didn't even know you were going to find out about it. It's just that us meeting in your room… I wasn't expecting it."

"And here you are, looking more confused and awkward than ever before. Not to mention that you just can't seem to stop looking down at my crotch," he mentioned and my cheeks grew beet-red. I didn't think that he was so perceptive, but I supposed that I should have known better.

He chuckled, circling me as if he was assessing everything that made me who I was.

"You are so stunning it's a wonder how you've remained a virgin this whole time," he murmured, stopping behind me when I thought that he was going to engulf me with his body again. And yet, that wasn't what happened. He took a couple more steps until he was in front of me again and stopped.

I was so confused about everything that was happening here

and I had no idea where it was all going to lead.

CHAPTER 3

"**S**gt. Frost..."

"Call me by my full name from now on," he said and it wasn't a request, but more like an order. And I was fine with that. If anything, I wanted to keep calling Sgt. Andrew Frost by his full name, including his rank and everything else, for the rest of my life. It helped to tickle the little part of me and it wasn't something that I was going to moan about. Not to mention that as a little that didn't experience much in terms of anything related to the universe, I should be taking advantage of this opportunity as much as possible.

"I'm sorry, Sgt. Andrew Frost. I was disrespectful and should be punished for that."

The moment I said that, he smirked. I thought he wasn't going to do anything close to that, but he decided to impress me. And that, in turn, made me notice a little twitch of something in his pants. I didn't want to think that it meant what it probably did, but there was no point in lying to myself.

"You should be. Do you want to be punished, Devin?" He asked, his eyes assessing me again. He looked so much more dominating, so much bigger than me, and thus it was so easy to keep falling into my little headspace, even though I was aware that I was still in the encampment and that any wrong step would probably mean the end of any career that I might think I could have here.

I nodded and he asked, "And do you know what kind of punishment you want?"

Was this really taking the direction that I was thinking it was?

I asked myself, my shaft giving little twitches in my pants. Before long, I was going to start seeping pre-come in my undies and there would be nothing I could do about that. He would notice what was going on and then he would think that I was a weirdo.

"Spanking," I said and my voice was throatier than it normally was, which was saying a lot. Ever since I turned 18, everyone always said that my voice sounded like that.

"Spanking, huh?" He said and then went over to his bed, where he sat on it. He waited a couple of seconds and when he realized that I wasn't moving, he patted his thigh vigorously, asking me to go there. But 'asking' was putting it mildly, I thought. It was more like he was demanding that I went there.

"Aren't you going to come?" He asked and there was no point in delaying the inevitable.

I went over to him and his eyes looked me up and down, almost as if he was showing that he was planning something sinful.

"Why are you still dressed?"

"I'm sorry?"

"Do you think that I should punish you even while you are still wearing your pants?" He asked and it made sense. I had no idea what I was even thinking, going to him while I was still with my clothes on.

He chuckled and I started to lower my pants, my heart pounding in my ears. I never thought that this moment was going to come, that I was going to be almost roleplaying with a possible Daddy, and that he was none other than Sgt. Andrew Frost himself.

When my pants were lowered and after I stepped out of them, he said, "You have such a nice pair of thin legs. I should put you through the grinder more from now on. Or maybe I like you too much the way you are."

"What?" I croaked again and it was so surreal everything that was going on in his room. Thankfully, the door was closed and nobody was going to come knocking on it, but still... I was almost role-playing as a little and this was like a dream come true.

My cheeks were beet red and my life was already like it was upside down.

"I was just saying that you are cute," he said, winking.

And after this was over, I had no idea what our coexistence here was going to be like.

I lied down over his legs, feeling his cock pressing against my belly. Sgt. Andrew Frost was hard and I never thought that he was going to be, especially not when he was with me. I supposed there was no point in hiding from the truth anymore. I didn't know if he was gay, but the fact was that he was getting off on this and wanted this to keep going on.

And from the looks of things, it seemed that his stick was quite big and thick. I was already imagining myself with my lips wrapped around it, loving it, kissing the tip of his cockhelmet, and I was pretty sure that he was thinking the same thing, too.

Sgt. Andrew Frost settled his hand on my ass, moving it around it, loving it. "You have such a perfect pair of asscheeks. I think I'm already getting addicted to it."

My cheeks were now even redder than before. I never thought that I was going to get such a compliment from the man himself.

He traced his finger across my ass crack, doing so slowly and painfully so. He was taking his time and the fact that he was doing that was so perfect I couldn't stop thinking about it. My whole body was beginning to shake over his lap.

"Are you afraid of this, recruit?" He asked, still roaming his hand over my ass, feeling every inch and part of it.

I nodded.

"You were naughty tonight. You jerked off without my permission and that is something I can't tolerate. Every time you even think about doing something like that, you have to ask for my permission, okay?"

I nodded again. It was the only thing I could keep doing right now, waiting until the punishment was inflicted on me.

"How many strikes do you think you should get for what you did?" He asked, still moving his hand around my ass so slowly it was almost like it was becoming one with it.

"I don't know..." I responded, and my dick was just so hard

right now, lust was everywhere in my body, and I couldn't stop the pre-come seeping through the slit of my cockhead. It was staining his pants and I was pretty sure that he was aware of that. And yet, he wasn't doing anything about that or even bringing it up.

"I think you should get 10," Sgt. Andrew Frost said and I knew that there was no point in arguing with him about it.

A moment later, his mind was made up and he delivered the first strike, right against my left ass cheek. I bit my bottom lip so hard I thought I was going to draw out blood, but it didn't happen. In the meantime, I was already having my first – or maybe I should be saying 'second' – orgasm. The first one happened before I came here and, from the looks of things, it appeared that I was going to have many more climaxes soon.

He chuckled, moving his other hand until it was under my junk and he started to play with it, focusing on my dickhead. "You're so excited. It's so great that you are. You are letting me explore you in every way I can."

I just nodded again, finding myself begging for my pacifier. I didn't bring one with me and I was certain that Sgt. Andrew Frost didn't have one with him, too, which was a pity.

He circled his hand around my ass and then lifted it, delivering a flurry of strikes on my butt. I felt like I was going to pass out, but I didn't in the end. The pain was just too much and it was everywhere in my body.

I was sweating all over and my asscheeks were stinging. Seconds went by and it started to feel better, but it still wasn't enough. I was just happy that it appeared that my punishment was over. Sgt. Andrew Frost must have noticed the smell of my come in the air when I entered his room. He was always perceptive, I noticed.

After a moment of nothingness, he said, "You were already thinking that it's over, right? It hardly is."

My eyes shot open at that same moment. I was almost falling asleep, barely in this moment, but now he snapped me right back into it.

"I thought that the punishment was already over, Daddy…" I

murmured, craning my head and trying to look at his eyes, finding how coldly he was staring at me now. It wasn't that he thought I was shit, but that he was always stern and determined when he needed to inflict punishments, especially on his recruits.

"There are still three strikes left," he said, moving his finger between my ass crack and then finding my asshole. He started to play and prod with it, making me close my eyes as pleasure surged in my body. It was everywhere, hitting every part of me and there was nothing that could be done about that. I was just loving the way he was playing with my rugged asshole and I wished he would never stop.

"I'm so ready to go inside of you when the time is right," he murmured, his other hand still stroking my dick. He wasn't doing that too fast. Rather, he was taking his time and I could feel how slick his hand was, thanks to the way that it got covered with my pre-come. Sgt. Andrew Frost was loving that, wasn't he?

"Please have mercy on me."

He cackled and I knew that meant he wasn't going to do that.

He lowered his head until I could feel his lips right by the side of my ear. "Do you believe that you deserve mercy, especially after doing something as naughty as jerking off while your roommates were sleeping around you?"

I gritted my teeth. Sgt. Andrew was right about that and that meant I had no excuses. And as if to punish me even more, he retreated his hand and I didn't feel his finger moving against my asshole anymore.

"Well, I guess it's time to finish your punishment," he affirmed and I knew that I had to ready myself for it. I felt his hand moving up in the air and then it stopped. He brought it down with force and slapped my asscheeks, though only a couple more times until the punishment was over.

When he was done, he settled his hand over my asscheek, moving it around it and massaging it. If it wasn't for that, I was pretty sure I'd be feeling a lot more pain than now and that was putting it mildly.

"That was almost too much," I said, and when I thought I was going to slide off his lap, he put his arms around me and picked me up. I was hugging him and even buried my head in the crook of his neck, which was a place that made me feel comfortable and that the punishment he just delivered was worth it.

His hand was massaging my back as he said over and over, "It's okay. You're going to be okay and as long as you behave yourself from now on, you don't have to worry about getting punished again."

And yet, I knew that I was going to be naughty just so that I could get spanked again. It was in my nature.

CHAPTER 4

I was holding the diaper in my hand and I didn't think I was going to be. The last thing I thought that could happen while I was in the Army was one of the Sergeants finding out that I was a little and that he was a Daddy. It was so great that he was, and now we were beginning to explore this side of our life. So much so that we were beginning to do something exciting today.

With the diaper now in my hands, I was beginning to wonder what we were going to do with it.

I was in the family bathroom and nobody could come in here, which was the only place where I had some privacy. I had to put on my diaper and then meet up with Sgt. Andrew Frost. I had no idea what he had in mind for me, but he said that I needed to go to his room again. I was presuming we were going to do something naughty and filthy, just like the first time, but that was still a mystery to me.

I took off my pants, put one leg through the hole in the diaper, and then the other, pulling it up. I connected both straps so that the diaper was secured on me, and I even turned and walked into the bathroom to make sure that it wasn't going to slide down.

Satisfied with that, I walked over to the mirror and checked myself out in it. I was still with my uniform shirt on and it perfectly fitted with the diaper. It made me feel like a combination of a soldier and a little, which was certainly not something I expected.

The diaper was thin and light enough to fit under the uniform's pants, I thought, picking it up and putting it on. I checked myself out one more time in the mirror, turning around again to make sure that the diaper wasn't creating a large volume. I didn't want anyone to find out that I was wearing it.

And one good thing about that was the fact that I felt so much safer and more comfortable to face the challenges that were going to come today. So much so that I even tipped up my chin, smoothed out my uniform, and felt handsome. I didn't just feel like my normal, boring self, but I felt hot. I felt I could make any gay man in the world fall to his knees before me.

I opened a smile after checking out to make sure that no part of the diaper was spilling out. I just couldn't go around in the en-campment fearing that someone was going to notice the diaper.

I walked through several hallways before finding myself in front of Sgt. Andrew Frost's door. I knocked on it and then he said, "Come on in, recruit."

I opened the door and found myself in his room. He was seated behind his desk just like last time and was scribbling something on a piece of paper. He was absorbed in it and wasn't paying any attention to me, which was a little disconcerting at first. And yet, I didn't let that phase me for too long. After all, the fact that Sgt. Andrew Frost asked me to come here meant that he wanted me to be here, that he thought I was important.

It wasn't going to be a repetition of what happened the first night we met.

He stood up then and started to walk around me, checking me out.

"You put your diaper on just like I requested that you did, didn't you?" He asked and I nodded.

"Good," he said, kissing my cheek and then putting his hands on my shoulders, moving them down until they were on my waist. I felt him feeling my diaper and I did nothing to stop him, mostly because he was arousing me beyond any level I thought possible. I was hard and ready to come, and yet I had to keep that from hap-pening. I didn't want to piss off Daddy like it happened that other time we were together. I wanted to be spanked sometimes, but not too often.

Today, I wanted to do something else.

"Come sit here with me," he said before stepping over to his bed, where he sat. He patted his thigh and I sat on his lap, doing exactly what he wanted. Even though I was padded, I could feel his hard and enraging dick poking through, and that was arousing me even more than I already was. I thought that it wasn't possible to feel like this without achieving my climax, but it was obvious that I could, as long as I was self-determined enough.

Sgt. Andrew Frost looped his arms around me, hugging me closely.

"I'm so happy that you followed everything I wanted to the letter," he said against my ear and it tickled me, making me feel goosebumps all over my body. He was always so proficient when doing this, always hitting every button that triggered me in a good way.

"Can I have my paci?" I asked and he shook his head left and right slowly. Sgt. Andrew Frost could always be so cruel when he wanted.

I pouted and even that wasn't enough to change his mind about it. He just chuckled, moving his hand over my belly and then under my diaper, finding my cock. He looped his fingers around it and started to massage my cockhead, which in turn made me turn my eyes so that I was looking at him, staring at his eyes, and then I parted my lips again.

"Daddy, you really aren't going to do this, or are you?" I asked and I knew that it was pointless that I was seeking an answer to that question. Whatever it was that he had in mind, he was going to do what he wanted.

And I could only go along with it.

CHAPTER 5

Sgt. Andrew Frost continued to apply pressure with his fingers on my cockhead, his fingers knowing exactly where to work, and where to do everything needed so that I felt the most amount of pleasure possible. It was almost too much and I was on the verge of coming. I could feel my heartbeat spiking, sweat coming out of the pores of my skin, and my dick throbbing.

"It's too much, Daddy," I said and I thought he was going to heed my plea, that he was going to give a damn to it, but it was pointless. He just kept on going, pressing and kneading my cockhead with his fingers and I knew I was going to hit my climax. And when that happened, I had no idea what his reaction would be like. I just hoped that he wouldn't be pissed off at me.

"It's too much for what?" He asked, nibbling on my earlobe and then kissing my neck, over and over, sometimes slowly and other times keeping his lips in touch with the skin there for periods longer than they needed to be. Sgt. Andrew Frost was relentless and he was turning me on so much that my skin was red.

It was going to happen. He was going to make me orgasm and I could do nothing to halt that. And the most striking thing about that was the fact that he wasn't even doing anything special, at least not much more than just moving his fingers professionally over my cockhead.

I closed my eyes and when I thought my milk was finally going to start spilling out, he opened his hand and stopped what he was doing. I felt the temperature of my body dropping, my heart rate slowing down, and everything else going back to normal.

I reopened my eyes slowly as I looked at him and asked without using words what happened.

"You thought it was going to be so easy?" He said, kissing my neck again and then one more time for good measure. I thought I was going to feel pissed off at him, but that wasn't what was in my heart right now.

I was a little disappointed, but I had felt that other times with other people, and I knew that it didn't mean much.

"I was almost going to come."

"That's why I stopped."

"Orgasm denial?" I asked, moving my hand over his arm and feeling how hard his muscles were. And not just that, but also that they followed curves and lines too difficult to put into words. I was pretty sure that, if I started working out and giving my all at the gym, I wouldn't have the same kind of body that he did. He was just perfect, out of this world, and I should be feeling thankful that he was always thinking about me and that we were roleplaying like this.

"It's a lot more than that," he responded, moving his finger along my bottom lip. He was always so sexy and teasing me like that, and there was nothing that could be done about that. He knew just how influential he was, especially when he was with me.

I started to move my hand over his thigh, looking for his crotch, but then he grabbed it and stopped it. I was, again, a little disappointed. If there was one thing I wanted to do with him right now, it was to jerk him off until he was coming all over me. I was always naughty like that and it would never change.

"Why are you so hard on me like this?" I asked, pouting.

"It's a lot more than that," he replied, purring against my neck and then grabbing a bottle of milk. I loved milk, especially when it was in a baby bottle, and I knew that he knew that too.

"Do you want some of this, little one?" He asked, putting the bottle right in front of my lips, teasing me. Sgt. Andrew Frost was always such a tease and that was never going to change about him, I thought.

I nodded and he put the teat of the bottle between my lips, and I wrapped them around it. It was as good as having a pacifier in my mouth and I knew that he knew that. So much so that I was already hard and excited again, feeling that now, unlike the first time, I could reach my orgasm without an issue. Even if Daddy stopped jerking me off with his hand, I would still come.

The formula that was in the bottle was tasty and slightly sugary, which was perfect for me. I kept on drinking it, as much as I could and for as long as possible. When it was almost empty, I was sad. I thought that there was a lot more milk in it.

He pulled the bottle away, checking me out with his piercing eyes. I had no idea what was going on in his mind, but I could still feel his hard cock pressing against my ass and I would do anything for this moment to last as long as possible.

I loved sitting on his lap and feeling his manhood against my orifice, even through the diaper.

"My belly is so full right now," I said, moving my hand around it.

"Do you want to mess your diaper?" He murmured against my ear, nibbling on my earlobe. Time was passing and I was supposed to be outside, training with the other soldiers, but it wasn't going to happen. Not as long as Sgt. Andrew Frost had me where he wanted me to be.

"Not right now," I responded and I knew that it was going to take some time, which was a pity. I wanted to mess my diaper and come in it too, but I knew that those things took time until they could happen.

"Then, go out and train. When you feel ready to do it, come here. I'm going to be waiting for you."

I blinked twice, not understanding what he meant. He wanted me to go out and pretend that nothing of this happened? Doing that was just impossible. I couldn't. Especially not now that I was all sweaty and my dick was still hard in my diaper. People were going to notice that something was amiss with me, and especially my friends could think that.

But then he pushed me off him and I was back on my feet. He

stood up, towering over me, and then patted me on the shoulder and made me go toward the door. I stopped in front of it as I asked him, without using words, what he was planning.

But then he gave me a serious, piercing look and I knew that I had to go along with whatever plan he had for me.

He opened the door and I stepped out. Just as I was walking away from his room, I heard him saying, "And don't forget to come here when you feel that you are close to messing your diaper."

And I did. I went to training, shot at targets, honed my shooting skills, and was then back in front of the door to his room. I knocked on it as I waited for him to invite me in. Time passed and nothing happened, which worried me, but then I noticed that the door was open by a crack.

I pushed it open and found myself inside his bedroom again. And when I noticed that Sgt. Andrew Frost was on his bed and stark naked, I halted right where I was. The last thing I thought I was going to see was him butt naked. His body was nothing short of perfect in every way I could think of and it aroused me more than anything else could.

"Sergeant, what's happening?" I asked, stepping toward him, but doing so awkwardly and while measuring each of my footsteps. The truth was that I had no idea what was going to happen now. I figured that he might finally breach me with his mighty cock and take my virginity, but even then that was only a possibility.

"Are you finally ready to mess your diaper, little one?" He asked, his fingers looping around his dick and then starting to stroke it. I noticed that, even though it was flaccid, it was still bigger and thicker than mine. It wasn't something I thought I was going to find out now, and not especially this evening.

I nodded and then he sat up on his bed, inviting me to sit on his lap. Doing that while he was clothed was already hot and doing the same now that he was naked was going to be even more so.

I wasn't just ready to mess my diaper – I was prepared to come in it, too.

CHAPTER 6

"You're always so obedient and ready to do everything I want," he said and I sat on his lap, feeling his hard-on pressing against my diaper. I was holding my pee until he said that I could mess my diaper. Until then, nothing was going to happen, I reminded myself. Even though I liked being spanked, I wasn't going to be naughty when my Daddy wanted me to be obedient.

"I strive to be your perfect little," I said and he smiled without showing his teeth, moving his hand under my uniform's shirt and then pulling it up and over my head. My torso was naked and all I could feel was his hand against my skin, loving how calloused it felt. It showed that Sgt. Andrew Frost was someone that went through a lot before finding himself here.

If there was something that always aroused me, it was hardened and strong men, and he fitted the bill perfectly.

"Can I mess my diaper?" I asked, hoping that he was going to say the magical word.

"What do you want to do first? Do you want to mess your diaper or do you want to come in it?"

"I want to do both things."

"But we can't do them at the same time. You have to pick one."

I pouted and when he saw that, he pressed his fingers against my lips, as if he was reprimanding me.

"Pouting isn't going to work right now against me. I'm not going to feel pity for you."

He moved his finger away and widened his smile.

And even though I wasn't going to say anything, I just decided to let it all out. My pee started to come out and mess my diaper, which was exactly what Sgt. Andrew Frost, my Big, was looking for. Even the glint of satisfaction in his eyes was telling. He loved that and it showed me that I made the right decision.

He moved his hand around the front of the diaper, feeling it.

"It's so heavy and soiled. You really were holding a lot until now, weren't you?" He said, his dick giving little twitches under the diaper. I could only imagine what I was going to feel like when I looped my fingers around his hardness, feeling it for everything that it was.

I nodded and that seemed to make him even happier than he was. So much so that he decided to say, "I'm not going to change your diaper now, but there is something that we can do before I have to do that."

"And what thing is that?" I asked, wishing that he could kiss me, but finding it obvious that he wasn't going to. The only thing that he appeared to be interested in was keeping me doing everything he wanted.

"Suck me off, but don't make me come just yet," he ordered and pushed me off him, and then I was back with my feet on the floor.

He spread his legs as he grabbed his cock again, showing it to me. Even though his hand was big, it looked small in comparison to the size of his dick. So much so that I was impressed and my mouth was salivating. The last thing I thought was going to happen now was that he was going to let me suck him off. I thought it was going to take a lot more time until that happened.

I was still on my knees and my hands were shaking. I put them on his thighs and started to massage and knead his skin, noticing how hairy his legs were. I already knew that they were like that, but feeling my hands moving over his leg hair was still something different than anything I thought possible.

His dick was right in front of me and I was nervous. I didn't think that I had the experience and the skills that he was seeking. When he realized that I didn't know how to give him head properly, he would be pissed.

"First time?" He asked and my heart went still. I knew that he was going to eventually figure it out, but I never thought he was going to be so blunt about it. One moment he was stroking his dick and the next he was dropping that bomb on me. I thought that he was going to be more delicate about it.

I could only nod right now. Just like all other times, there was no point in hiding the truth.

"Don't worry about it. Take your time, don't use your teeth, and do use your tongue. Remember the part under my cockhead. It's where it's more sensitive."

I knew that those tips were simple, but it was still difficult for me to keep them in mind. I just decided to lower my head, close my eyes, and widen my mouth as wide as it could go. In no moment at all, his cockhead was in my mouth and I was already beginning to worship it, even though it wasn't sufficient.

I knew that more needed to be done.

And I was already so happy with myself when he tilted his head backward and closed his eyes, a little moan of pleasure escaping his lips. I thought that my inexperience was going to get in the way, that he was going to get annoyed by that, but it appeared that wasn't the case. So much so that I was even beginning to grow more confident and started to play with his balls, tugging at them and feeling them.

"Ooooh, fuck. That's it. Keep that up," he murmured over and over, giving me more confidence and I, in turn, couldn't stop doing what I was doing. I kept on sucking him off, giving him everything that he needed, and I knew that he was going to come inside my mouth. And when that happened, I would swallow all of his come.

And just when I was getting used to it, he put his hand on my head and pulled it away, which made me blink twice in confusion. I pouted and asked, "I thought you were enjoying it."

"I was. It's just not the time for that yet. Plus, I was lying when I said that I wanted you to make me come – or did I even say that?" He said, turning his eyes to the upper right and making me wonder what was even going on in his head.

He waved his hand as he chuckled and then he said, "It doesn't matter. What matters right now is changing your diaper. You messed it so much that it's already all smelly and looking a little gross."

I thought that he was going to punish me, to make me wear my diaper for a lot longer than I should, but it appeared that he had other plans in mind. He grabbed me, made me lie down on his bed, and then lowered my diaper. It was messy and smelled a lot, too.

"Oh, look at the mess you made," he said, stepping away from me and then tossing the soiled and messy diaper in his trash bin. He closed it and came back to me.

"I think that, first, you need to shower. You smell so much that just cleaning you now with baby wipes wouldn't be enough."

He grabbed me again, took me to the bathroom, and then turned on the showerhead. I stepped under it, feeling the water moving around my body. I closed my eyes and thought of nothing until I felt his arms coming from behind me and looping around me.

I flinched and was shocked that he did that, but when he tightened his arms around me, I knew that everything was cool and okay. I could feel his body making mine feel so much smaller and it wasn't even the tip of the iceberg of everything else that he was making me feel.

I could feel his cock pressing against my ass. Then, he grabbed a bath sponge and started to move it around my body, soaping up my skin. The water rinsed it right away and, in no time at all, I was feeling clean and much better than before.

And, especially now that his naked body was pressing against mine from behind, I was much more aroused. So much so that my pre-come was seeping through the slit of the cockhead and I knew that more was going to come.

He put the bath sponge where he got it from and then started to explore my body with his hands, focusing on my nipples. He was exciting them and, in turn, I could only close my eyes and feel my dick getting harder. It was so hard right now I feared that it would never go back to normal.

"Are you ready for your first time, to finally lose your virginity?" He murmured against my ear, moving his finger in my ass crack and then looking for my asshole. When he was rubbing it with his finger, I knew that he wasn't going to stop there and that giving any answer different from the one he was looking for would be suicide.

"Yes, Daddy," I replied and he took a step away from me, putting his hand on my back and then bending me over. The showerhead was still turned on and I could feel the water hitting my back, moving around it.

"Stay like that and don't move. There's something that I need to get," Sgt. Andrew Frost said before moving away from me and doing something in the other part of his room. I had no idea what it was that he did, but he appeared to have grabbed something and then quickly came back to me while holding it in his hand.

I peeked over my shoulder as I noticed what it was. It was a bottle of lube, which he was already pouring on his hand, and he used it to oil up his dick. It looked shiny under the light hanging from the ceiling. Shiny and ready to penetrate me until nothing was left of me, I thought.

"I'm not going to be gentle, just so you know," he warned and one of the things that told me he was right about that was the fact that my back was hurting, he was aware of that, and he wasn't doing anything about it.

He was even taking his time oiling up his dick. In the meantime, I just couldn't wait until he was inside of me and was creaming in there.

"And I told you I'm not going to hurry up," he affirmed, moving toward me with his hand oiled up. He started to move his fingers on my orifice and then in my rectum, lubing up those regions. When he figured that it was ready, he put the bottle of lube on the floor and took another step toward me. This time, I could feel his veiny and raging dick pressing against the lower side of my ass, and it was one of the most arousing feelings of my life.

"I'm coming in now and I hope you are ready for it," he said before nudging my orifice with his stick and then breaching through the initial barrier, stretching me beyond any level I thought possible. His dick was just so thick, so big, and I feared he couldn't fit it inside of me. I was so sure about it that I was in shock when I found out that he managed to put all of it inside of me.

"Shit, I can only see my balls right now," he murmured, his hands on my waist and gripping it with confidence. His fingers dug into my skin as he started to roll his hips and was doing that slowly, which was a surprise to me. I thought that he was going to be at maximum speed from the get-go.

I could feel his balls slapping against my ass and it was the most thrilling and exciting thing that ever happened in my life. So much so that my dick started to unload my come all over the floor and the water of the showerhead, and I tracked it as it was pushed down the drain.

I never thought that I was going to have my first time while I was in my little mode, and it was so great that it was happening like this. My heart was pounding, sweat was coming out of my pores, and I could still feel the water moving around my body.

The combination of everything that was happening was enough to make me reach my orgasm and I came for what felt like hours, but I was pretty sure that they were nothing more than minutes. When I was done, I was panting and I just noticed that he was still ramming in and out of me, and feeling that was enough to make me climax one more time.

Minutes later, he was creaming inside of me and I could feel his milk filling my rectum. So much so that I wasn't surprised when some of it started to spill out. I was only saddened that I couldn't do anything about that. If there was something I wanted to do, it was to make sure that every single drop of it remained inside of me.

Then, he slowly pulled out, turned off the showerhead, and went with me where the sink was. He dried me with a towel, put a new diaper on me, and then lied down with me on his bed. Sgt. Andrew Frost didn't say anything and was just moving his hand over my head, caressing my cheek.

"You did well. You are my forever little one from now on, and I'm going to take you out of here after your training is over."

After spending so much energy on our sex, the only thing I could do was to keep my eyes open for as long as possible, but even then that wasn't enough. I was soon asleep and Sgt. Andrew Frost was snoring.

I couldn't wait for what else he had in store for me and I knew that it was going to be thrilling.

The End

Looking for more ABDL MM? Check out these top series starters:

1. Firefighter's Punished Little
2. My Caring Biker
3. Be my ABDL

And leave your **review**! I love reading your feedback.

TEASER: MY CARING BIKER

ABDL MM Biker Romance (Sweet Pacis – 1)

Carson

I kicked a bottle, watching as it rolled across the sidewalk. I heard the annoying sound of their motorcycles coming before they were close enough to annoy me. If there was one thing I couldn't stand, it was a Harley-Davidson. I felt like the noise of it was impaling my ears.

I covered them when they blasted past me, with some of them turning their heads at me and staring at me through their sunglasses.

We were in Houston and I was aware that the sun was hot today, as usual, but I still found their sunglasses corny as hell.

I was walking down the street with my head low, thinking about life. I was in college, studying History, and thinking that I was wasting my time. I mean, what was I thinking it was going to be for? That companies were looking to hire students like me?

In truth, I was lost. I didn't think that I was going to get rich off that degree, which was why I wasn't studying for my upcoming midterms. My professors were going to scold me for this.

They thought I was busting my ass off. They either couldn't notice that I was having a severe case of depression, or they were too blind to even think that was a major problem nowadays.

And I wasn't going to see a therapist about that because I didn't have the money. I supposed that it was a good thing that at least my parents were paying for my stay here.

They didn't know that I had a secret I couldn't share with them. When nobody was looking, I was a little. I put on a onesie, socks, and crawled around in the room I slept in.

I couldn't do that often, though. I lived in a suite, but I had suitemates in other rooms, and they would make me the talk of the town if they found out about my secret.

That's why dating was even harder for me. How could I date someone that would look at my littleness and think that I was odd? I couldn't take the risk. If I did, my whole life would be ruined.

Not to mention that I wouldn't be able to continue keeping it hidden from my family. They would disown me. I'd have to delete all of my social media accounts, which I already didn't have many of anyway.

I didn't want people to find out about my littleness. The photos I uploaded on those websites, I showed to a select group of people only. My friends and one or another family member that was open-minded enough.

I thought that I despised all bikers equally, but there was one of them, leading the small horde that was in tow, who looked at me as if he thought there was something wrong with me. I hated him even more.

In comparison to him, I was nothing. Too small and insignificant, though it did feel like he was feeling something... different for me? I wasn't going to pretend that I could read his mind or do something of the sort...

Terry

I did see a short, weak man walking with a hunched posture and his head lowered. From a distance, I didn't pay much attention to him. I was riding with my friends and we were having a good time. I couldn't have asked for anything better for this evening.

We didn't live here in Houston. We were nomads, though we decided to stay here for the time being. We thought that this was a good place to meet like-minded people.

There was a stigma surrounding bikers, and even though we didn't plan on changing that, we wanted to bring more people to the club.

I'd gotten off my bike and talked with my biker colleagues. Our motorcycle club was called the Spectral Rats MC, and we usually spent our time talking about motorcycles, how to make them better, and doing whatever we could to make money.

More often than not that meant doing the odd job here and there, but other times that meant riding in some night races. I knew that the police didn't like them.

Not to mention that it was… kind of outlawed. I wasn't straight up going to say that they were, but most of the law said that we couldn't have races at night.

I tried not to think too much about that. Mom and dad didn't like me at all. They were very conservative and voted only for conservative politicians. The country was still in a large turmoil thanks to them.

Our camp wasn't anything to write home about. We had our tents, a campfire in the middle of it, and bikers sitting on logs and telling tales of their adventures.

Beers were a constant in our lives, too. Cans were scattered around the camp, which was located just outside of Houston. Most people didn't look with kind eyes to bikers like us. They thought that we were trash.

I didn't miss my parents and the rest of my family at all. If anything, I was happy we didn't have to see each other again. And they were more than glad they didn't have to include me in their will when they passed away.

Gosh, that was such a horrible thought. Good thing I didn't have to be reminded of it all the time. I had my own life now, with this biker gang I now called my new family.

My mind was still going back to that little guy. He couldn't be more than 20 years old. Here, in my family, everybody knew that I was gay. They didn't have a problem with it, and that only made me feel more at home here.

I did have a couple of boyfriends in my life, and neither of them made me feel complete.

Not to its fullest extent. Now that I was 30, I was already thinking that finding love wasn't going to happen to me.

I did have a nagging feeling that guy might be in danger, though. With the sun already setting, what did he think he was doing at night? I knew that he was an adult.

I was aware of that, but I still felt that I needed to check out what was happening there.

I knew that, most likely, he wasn't even going to be there anymore, but who said that I was only going to do that? I was also thinking about going to the nearest McDonalds to buy a burger for dinner...

OTHER MM ABDL BOOKS

SERIES - BROKEN LITTLES

1. Rockstar's Little: Halloween Romance
2. Doctor's Little: Halloween Romance
3. Biker's Little for Christmas: Stuck Together MC
4. Rockstar's Little for Christmas: Secret Relationship
5. Quarterback's Little: Rejected Marriage
6. Stalker's Sweet Little: ABDL MM Romance

SERIES - REGRESSED

1. Gifting Crayons: ABDL MM Romance
2. Sugar Mister: ABDL MM Romance
3. Loving Little Chris: ABDL MM Romance
4. Bedtime for Cody: ABDL MM Romance
5. Little Crayons: ABDL MM Romance

ABOUT THE AUTHOR

Jerry Hastings

Jerry Hastings biggest love? Writing MM ABDL books. He can't go a day without imagining worlds where littles find their Daddies and live their HEAs. His stories are peppered with diapers, pacis, and coloring books.

His best-sellers are 'Quarterback's Little' and 'My Caring Biker', which are books that he'll always remember fondly. You can find them on his author page.